Gifted & Talented®

More Questions & Answers

For Ages 4–6

By Bailey Kennedy, M.S.

Illustrated by Larry Nolte

Lowell House
Juvenile
Los Angeles

CONTEMPORARY BOOKS
Chicago

To my family, for their continual love and support
—BK

Reviewed and endorsed by Dr. Anthony D. Fredericks, author of many
adult and juvenile titles including *The Gifted Reader Handbook,*
The Science Discovery Book, *Weird Walkers*, and *Exploring the Rainforest.*

ISBN: 1-56565-504-4

Library of Congress Catalog: 96-27297

Publisher: Jack Artenstein
Associate Publisher, Juvenile Division: Elizabeth D. Amos
Director of Publishing Services: Rena Copperman
Managing Editor: Lindsey Hay
Editor in Chief, Nonfiction: Amy Downing
Project Editor: Jessica Oifer
Art Director: Lisa-Theresa Lenthall

Lowell House books can be purchased at special discounts
when ordered in bulk for premiums and special sales.
Contact Department JH at the following address:
Lowell House Juvenile
2029 Century Park East, Suite 3290
Los Angeles, CA 90067

Manufactured in the United States of America

10 9 8 7 6 5 4 3 2 1

Note to Parents

Teach a child facts and you give her knowledge. Teach her to think and you give her wisdom. This is the principle behind the entire series of Gifted and Talented® materials. And this is the reason that thinking skills are becoming stressed widely in classrooms throughout the country.

The questions and answers in the **Gifted & Talented® Question & Answer** books have been designed specifically to promote the development of critical and creative thinking skills. Each page features one "topic question" that is answered next to a corresponding picture. This topic provides the springboard to the following questions on the page.

Each of the six questions focuses on a different higher-level thinking skill. The skills include knowledge and recall, comprehension, deduction, inference, sequencing, prediction, classification, analyzing, problem solving, and creative expansion.

The topic question, answer, and artwork contain the answers or clues to the answers for some of the other questions. Certain questions, however, can only be answered by relating the topic to other facts that your child may know. In the back of the book are suggested answers to help you guide your child.

Effective questioning has been used to develop a child's intellectual gifts since the time of Socrates. Certainly, it is the most common teaching technique in classrooms today. But asking questions isn't as easy as it looks! Here are a few tips to keep in mind that will help you and your child use this book more effectively:

★ First of all, let your child flip through the book and select the questions and pictures that interest him or her. Unlike most books, this book does not have to be read consecutively. Each page is totally self-contained. Start at the back, the front, the middle—the choice is up to your child!

★ If your child wants to do only one page, that's great. If he or she only wants to answer some of the questions on a page, save the others for another time.

★ Give your child time to think! Pause at least ten seconds before you offer any help. You'd be surprised how little time many parents and teachers give a child to think before jumping right in and answering a question themselves.

★ Help your child by restating or rephrasing the question if necessary. But again, make sure you pause and give the child time first. Also, don't ask the same question over and over! Go on to another question, or use hints to prompt your child when needed.

★ Encourage your child to give more details or expand answers by asking questions such as "What made you say that?" or "Why do you think so?"

★ This book will not only teach your child about many things, but it will teach *you* a lot about your child. Make the most of your time together—and have fun!

The answers in the back of the book are to be used as a guide. Sometimes your child may come up with an answer that is different but still a good answer. Remember, the principle behind all *Gifted and Talented*® materials is to **teach your child to think**—not just to give answers.

What makes the sound of thunder?

The sound of thunder is caused by the heat of a lightning flash. The electricity in a lightning flash is so hot it makes the loud roar we hear. The closer a thunderstorm is to you, the louder it sounds.

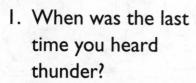

1. When was the last time you heard thunder?
2. What can you do to keep yourself safe and not scared during a thunderstorm?
3. When there is a thunderstorm during the day, what do you see?
4. If you were drawing a picture of a thunderstorm, how would you show the loud noise thunder makes?
5. Why do you think people say that a herd of running elephants sounds like thunder?
6. Make up a story about a storm giant named Thunderhead. How would Thunderhead look, sound, and act?

What are goose bumps?

When people are cold or frightened, they get goose bumps. There is a little muscle attached to every single hair on our bodies. When we feel cold or afraid, each tiny hair muscle contracts, or shrinks, and pulls the hair straight up. As the hair rises up, it pulls on the skin and forms a little bump. We call this a *goose bump* because it looks like the skin of a goose without its feathers.

1. Have you ever seen goose bumps on your arms or legs? Do they hurt?
2. What else happens to your body when you are scared or really cold?
3. What do you think people mean when they say, "You have a goose egg on your head"?
4. On a separate piece of paper, draw a picture of yourself with goose bumps.
5. What do you think a gooseneck lamp looks like?
6. Make up a scary story that will give people goose bumps.

❓ Why do magnets stick to the refrigerator?

Magnets are made of iron. They are attracted to, or will stick to, metal objects that have iron or steel in them. Magnets stick to your refrigerator because your refrigerator has steel or iron inside of it.

1. Why might a magnet stick to another magnet?
2. Point to the things in the picture that you think a magnet will stick to or pick up.
3. Why will a magnet repel, or not pick up, some items?
4. Will a magnet stick to your oven door? Why or why not?
5. What does it mean when someone is "magnetic"?
6. If you were a magnet, what things would you feel most attracted to in your home?

One Step Further
Ask an adult to help you find a magnet that you can use. Then test your magnet around your home. Draw a picture of all the things your magnet picked up. How many items did you draw? What did your magnet repel?

Where does honey come from?

Honey is made by the smallest bees, the female workers. These bees fly to flowers and use their tongues to suck the flowers' sweet juice called *nectar*. When they have gathered enough nectar, they fly back to their beehive to make the honey that they store in honeycombs. This is called "making a beeline."

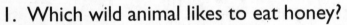

1. Which wild animal likes to eat honey?
2. Would you comb your hair with a honeycomb? Why or why not?
3. Why do some people call other people "honey"?
4. What do you think a beekeeper does?
5. What does it mean when someone says, "Make a beeline for the playground"?
6. Have you ever spread honey on toast? How does honey taste? How does it feel when you touch it?

What makes a candle melt?

Heat or hot temperatures cause some solid things to melt, soften, or change to a liquid. When a candle is lit, the hot flame softens the candle wax closest to it. As the flame burns, the candle melts. Sometimes the melted wax drips down the side of the candle.

1. With your finger, circle all the things in the picture that can melt.
2. What happens to a candle as it melts?
3. What happens to butter when you spread it on your hot toast or pancakes? Why?
4. Have you ever eaten an ice-cream cone that started to melt? What happened to the ice cream in your cone?
5. What is the opposite of melting?
6. If snow is cold when you touch it, why does a snow person melt?

Which animals have pockets on their bodies?

Animals with pockets, or pouches, on their bodies are called *marsupials*. Kangaroos, koalas, and opossums (commonly known as possums) are all marsupials. These pouched animals are mammals just like us. When a baby marsupial is born, it is very, very tiny. The baby crawls into its mother's pouch, where it can stay safe and warm until it is ready to live in the outside world. As baby marsupials get bigger, they spend more and more time outside their mothers' pouches. For example, a baby koala clings to its mother's back when it is too big for her pouch.

1. Have you ever seen a marsupial? Which one did you see?
2. What do kangaroos and their babies eat? How do they get around? Use the picture on the opposite page as a clue.
3. Which marsupial mother and baby look like cuddly teddy bears? What does this family eat?
4. In what country do kangaroos and koalas live?

5. How many marsupials do you see in both pictures? If kangaroos have two legs and koalas and opossums have four legs, how many legs are there altogether?

6. On a separate piece of paper, draw your own picture of marsupials. Where will these marsupials live? Where will you draw their babies?

One Step Further

Imagine that you are a mother kangaroo. Put a backpack on backward, with the pouch in front! How do you act differently? What are things you like about your pocket? What don't you like about it?

What is fog?

Fog is a very thick mist or cloud made up of tiny drops of water that stay close to the ground. A fog cloud is formed when moisture rises up from the warm earth into the colder air. When a fog cloud is very thick or dense, it is hard to see through.

1. When was the last time you walked in fog?
2. What does fog look and feel like?
3. Why do you think it is dangerous to drive a car or ride a bike in heavy fog?
4. What does it mean when an airport is "fogged in"?
5. When someone says, "My mind is in a fog today!" and it's a sunny day, what does that person mean?
6. How would you draw a picture of a foggy day?

What are junk foods?

Junk foods are foods that may taste good, but don't give us enough vitamins and minerals to stay strong and healthy. Some junk foods have lots of sugar in them, like cookies and ice cream. Others have lots of fat, like pepperoni and french fries. To stay healthy, you should eat lots of fresh fruits and vegetables, as well as cereals and pasta.

1. Point to all the junk foods in the picture. Why do you think they are called junk foods?
2. Name all the healthy foods you can find in the picture.
3. On a separate piece of paper, draw a picture of your favorite healthy foods. Why do you like these foods?
4. Plan a pretend junk food party for you and a friend. List all the junk foods you would have at this party.
5. How would you feel if you ate all the junk foods at your pretend party?
6. Make up a story about a tug-of-war game between the Healthy Food Hunks and the Junk Food Bandits.

How do flies walk on the ceiling?

Flies have tiny pads on their feet. Some scientists think these pads are sticky and help flies hold on to the ceiling. Other scientists think that the pads stick to the ceiling the same way a suction cup holds on to something. Either way, the pads on their feet allow flies to walk on the ceiling.

1. Have you ever seen a fly walking on your ceiling? How did it stay up there?
2. On a separate piece of paper, draw a picture of how your bedroom would look from a fly's view if it was on your ceiling.
3. What is a housefly? Where do you think it lives?
4. If you used a magnifying glass to look at a fly, what would you see?
5. What animals eat flies?
6. Tell a funny story about the Fly Family whose members spend most of their lives living upside down on a ceiling.

Why do we have to sleep?

We have to sleep so our muscles, including our brains, can rest. After a day of activity, our bodies get tired and need time to restore energy. Our brains also need to rest because they work all day long.

1. What types of things help you get ready to go to sleep? Look for clues in the picture.
2. Do you sleep with your eyes open or closed? Do you sleep in the same position all night?
3. How many hours do you sleep every night?
4. What does it mean to feel drowsy?
5. Why is it hard to sleep if you feel excited or scared?
6. How do you feel when you don't get enough sleep?

Why do some things float and other things sink?

If an object weighs less than the water surrounding it, it will float. An object will sink, or go below the surface of the water, if it weighs more than the water around it. So even very heavy objects can sometimes float. Also, certain objects filled with a lot of air may float because air weighs less than water.

1. Look at the picture. Which objects will float on the surface of the water?

2. Name all the objects in the picture you think will sink. How many did you name?

3. How can people float on top of the water in a swimming pool, lake, or the ocean?

4. What other words can you think of that rhyme with **float?** Do you think any of these things float?

5. What words rhyme with **sink?**

6. What is a floating island? What do you think it might look like?

One Step Further

Ask an adult to help you put some water in a large pan or tub. Collect some things that you think will float and some things that you think will sink. Write down which things you think will float and sink. Test your guesses. Were you right? Draw one picture of the objects that floated and another picture of the objects that sank.

What causes hiccups?

You can get hiccups when you swallow a lot of air or a big gulp of food at one time. If too much air rushes into your lungs, the opening of your windpipe quickly snaps shut to stop any more air from entering. This makes the funny-sounding "hic" noise, which may last for several minutes. If your breathing muscle moves up and down too fast, you also may get hiccups.

1. Have you ever had hiccups? How do they feel?
2. Why are the children in the picture laughing?
3. How can you stop hiccups?
4. If you put your hand on the chest of someone who is having hiccups, what do you think it will feel like?
5. How is a hiccup different from a cough?
6. Make up a story about the people on Hiccup Hill who try lots of funny tricks to get rid of their hiccups.

How did fairy tales get their name?

Fairy tales got their name because they are stories, or tales, about fairies, wizards, giants, or other characters who have magical or unusual powers. They are fictional stories that were created many, many years ago by great storytellers. Fairy tales may have people with incredible powers, animals that talk, or an enchanted, or magical, forest.

1. What fairy tale do you like best of all? Why?
2. How do you know fairy tales are make-believe?
3. Think of your favorite fairy tale. Which parts of that story could happen in real life?
4. If you made up your own fairy tale, what kind would you create? Would your characters be spooky or enchanted?
5. On a separate piece of paper, draw a picture of one fairy-tale character you would create.
6. Write a postcard to your favorite fairy-tale character. Be sure to include an enchanted address.

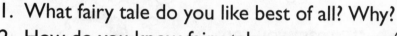

Why do we dream?

Dreaming happens after we fall into a deep sleep. It is one way our brains sort out all the things that have happened to us in the past few days. Dreams are like many strange stories that get all mixed together. In just one dream you may have lots of different thoughts and see many different images.

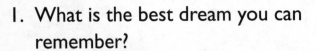

1. What is the best dream you can remember?
2. On a separate piece of paper, draw a picture of what a dream might look like.
3. What is daydreaming? How are daydreams different from other dreams?
4. What is the child in the picture daydreaming about?
5. What are nightmares? Have you ever had a nightmare? How did it make you feel?
6. Create a story about Dream Town, where the Sweet Dreams Family and the Nightmare Family live. How will each family look and act?

Do trees breathe like people do?

No, trees don't breathe as we do. They breathe in their own way—through their leaves that absorb, or take in, the gas carbon dioxide. People and animals exhale carbon dioxide as they breathe out. Trees need carbon dioxide, water, and sunshine to grow. As they grow, trees give off oxygen, a gas people and animals breathe in.

1. How are the children in the picture using a tree for fun?
2. How do trees help human beings?
3. On a separate piece of paper, draw a picture of all the foods you can think of that grow on trees.
4. Which animals eat parts of a tree? What do they eat?
5. Name as many animals as you can that live in trees.
6. What kinds of trees grow where you live? How could you find out what the trees are called?

How do some wild animals hide from danger?

Many wild animals hide, or camouflage, themselves from their enemies with the protective coloring of their skin or fur. The animals have colors or markings that look very much like the surroundings they live in. When these wild animals stay quiet and stand very still, you can hardly see them.

1. How does a tiger's markings help camouflage it?
2. Which wildcats have spots on their fur to help them blend into their surroundings?
3. Why do you think female birds do not have bright, colorful feathers like male birds?
4. Can you think of other animals that have coloring that helps to hide them?
5. If you were camouflaged in the snow, what would you be wearing?
6. What colors would you wear to hide in a tree?

What are taste buds?

There are over 10,000 tiny cells all over your tongue that help you taste the different flavors in your food. Small groups of these cells are called *taste buds*. Your taste buds are located in between the many small bumps on your tongue. Different parts of your tongue have different types of taste buds that help you taste salty, sweet, sour, and bitter flavors.

1. What is your favorite taste? Why?
2. What part of your tongue tastes sour lemon juice? What part tastes salty potato chips? Use the picture as a clue.
3. What do you think it means when someone says, "This food is really tasty"?
4. Why do some people put salt, pepper, or sugar on their food? What part of your tongue tastes sugar?
5. What does it mean when someone says you have good taste in clothes?
6. Pretend you are a taste bud. What kind of taste bud would you be? How would you act when you taste food you don't like?

How are our shadows made?

When the sun or a light shines on you, a shadow may be created. A *shadow* is a shaded area that appears in your shape when you sit or stand between a light source and a surface, like a wall or the ground. The size of your shadow changes depending on how far you are from the light source.

1. What are the children in the picture doing?
2. How can you make a shadow of yourself?
3. Will you see shadows outside on a cloudy day? Why or why not?
4. Why do some children get scared at night when they see shadows on their bedroom walls?
5. What does it mean when someone says, "He (or she) is like my shadow"?
6. On a separate piece of paper, draw shadows that would form at a playground filled with children on a sunny day.

One Step Further

Go outdoors and find your shadow. Ask an adult to help you measure your shadow at different hours of the day. Does your shadow look the same in the morning, at lunch, and late in the afternoon? Why or why not?

Do cows lie down when they sleep?

Adult cows sometimes lie down to sleep, but they do not have to. They can close their eyes and sleep while standing. But if they are hot, tired of standing, or sometimes if a storm is coming, they may lie down. Often baby cows, called *calves*, sleep close to each other while lying down near their mothers.

1. Have you ever seen a cow lying down? Where do you think you might see one?
2. How big are cows? What colors are they?
3. What is another name for a group of cows that live together?
4. Why are cows important farm animals?
5. How do you think cows keep insects such as flies from landing on and bothering them?
6. Did you know that you have calves on your body? Where are they? How many calves do you have?

ZZZZZZ!

What do our skeletons do?

Your body is made up of 206 bones. Together, all your bones form your skeleton, which holds up, supports, and protects everything inside your body. Just like a house needs a wood frame to hold it up, your body needs your skeleton to stand up.

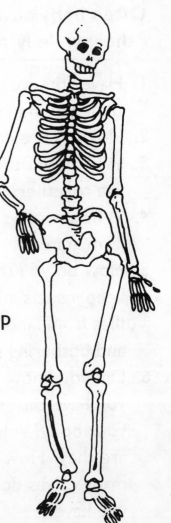

1. What would happen to a house if it lost its frame?
2. Point to these bones on the skeleton in the picture.
   - the jawbone
   - the shinbone
   - the backbone
   - the collarbone
   - the thighbone
   - the anklebone
3. What is the name of the largest bone in your head?
4. What is the name of the machine that takes pictures of your bones?
5. Why do you think some children dress up as skeletons on Halloween?
6. What does it mean when someone says, "You're all skin and bones"?

Why do we bleed when we cut ourselves?

When we cut ourselves, blood vessels in our skin are opened and we bleed. A cut heals as the blood dries up and forms a clot that covers the cut. This clot then becomes a hard scab. When a scab falls off, you will see the new, healthy skin that has grown under it.

1. What happened to the child in the picture? What is the grown-up doing?
2. When was the last time you cut yourself? How did it happen? What did your cut look like? How did it feel?
3. Even if it itches, why should you try not to scratch a scab?
4. Have you ever seen yellow stuff called *pus* ooze out of a cut? What do you think makes this pus?
5. What happens when a cat or dog cuts itself?
6. Why do you think people wear bandages on their cuts?

❓ Why do we recycle things?

Recycling is one important way we can protect the earth, keep it clean, and cut down the amount of trash that is thrown away and never used again. People recycle all kinds of things such as aluminum cans, glass and plastic bottles, newspapers, and even old tires. When objects are recycled, they can be made into new objects and used again.

1. How are the children in the picture helping to protect the environment?
2. If you had some old, stale bread at your house that you could not eat, how could you recycle it?
3. What could you do to help keep our planet clean by recycling things at your house?
4. How could old car or truck tires be recycled?
5. How many items can you find around your house that are made of recycled material? As a clue, look for the recycle symbol with arrows in a circle or a recycle message.
6. What special T-shirt could you design about recycling? On a separate piece of paper, draw a picture of what your T-shirt would look like and what it would say.

One Step Further
Ask an adult to help you make puppets from recycled things in your house. You could create a scary monster with egg-carton teeth, or a funny paper-bag elephant with floppy newspaper ears and a cardboard-tube trunk. After you make your puppets, put on a puppet show and teach your friends and family how they can recycle, too.

What are the five senses?

Your body has five senses, which are ways to send messages to your brain. The five senses are touch, taste, sight, hearing, and smell. You smell through your nose and you taste through the taste buds on your tongue. You touch through the small nerve endings in your skin. Your eyes help you see, and your ears allow you to hear.

1. What part of your body do you use to touch? How do you hear?
2. When you play a game of tag with a friend, what senses do you use?
3. Pretend you are eating a crunchy apple. How many of your senses do you think are working? Why?
4. What sometimes happens to your sense of smell when you have a cold?
5. Which of your five senses do you think you use to learn how to do things?
6. On a separate piece of paper, draw a picture of you and your friends playing and using all five of your senses.

Who gave dinosaurs such funny names?

When dinosaur fossils were first discovered almost 200 years ago, scientists used Greek words to name the different dinosaurs. A huge plant eater with a long, thin neck and a thick tail was named *Brontosaurus* (bron-tuh-SORE-us). It is now called *Apatosaurus* (uh-PAT-uh-sore-us). The most well-known meat-eating dinosaur was called *Tyrannosaurus rex* (ty-ran-oh-SORE-us recks).

1. Have you ever seen a dinosaur skeleton? Where did you see it? What did it look like? What was its name?
2. What other dinosaurs can you name?
3. Do you think people were living on earth when there were dinosaurs?
4. Dinosaurs were reptiles. What other reptiles can you name?
5. Where can you see reptiles living today?
6. Dinosaurs became extinct. What do you think this means?

Why do our noses run?

You always have a thin layer of watery, slimy stuff called *mucus* on the inside of your nose. This mucus traps the dirt and germs that are in the air you breathe. When you have a cold, extra mucus is made to help get rid of the cold germs. This mucus makes your head feel stuffy and your nose sometimes run.

On a really cold day, your nose also may run even if you aren't sick. The cold air causes the mucus to come together and form larger drops that make your nose run.

1. When was the last time your nose ran?
2. Does your runny nose run the same way you run down a soccer field? Why or why not?
3. How can you help a friend whose nose is running?
4. How is a runny nose like a dripping faucet?
5. Do you think animals ever get runny noses? Why or why not?
6. On a separate piece of paper, draw a funny picture of a runny nose running down the street.

How do cows make milk?

A dairy cow changes grass into milk as it moves the grass through the four parts of its stomach. In each part, it breaks the grass down into smaller and softer pieces. Eventually it becomes the milk we drink.

1. How do people get milk from a cow?
2. What foods are made with cow's milk?
3. When do you usually drink milk? With which foods do you like to drink milk?
4. What words can you think of that rhyme with **cow?**
5. How do you think the milk you drink gets from the cow to your glass?
6. What other animal besides a cow makes milk that people drink? Have you ever drunk milk from another animal?

Why do people's toes and fingers get wrinkled when they take a bath?

When you take a long bath, the water gently pulls moisture from the skin on the long, thin parts of your body. As the water is sucked out, your fingers and toes lose their plumpness. Your skin gets dry and wrinkled. It will look normal again after you've been dry for a little while.

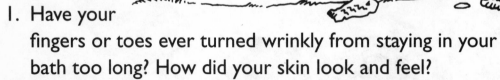

1. Have your fingers or toes ever turned wrinkly from staying in your bath too long? How did your skin look and feel?
2. Why are the children in the picture laughing? What have they been doing?
3. What foods have wrinkled-looking skins?
4. What happens to people's skin when they get older?
5. What do people do when their clothes wrinkle?
6. There is a Chinese dog called a *shar-pei* (shar-pay) that has lots of wrinkled skin. What do you think this dog looks like?

Where does sand come from?

Sand comes from pieces of crumbled rocks. Water and wind break larger rocks into smaller rocks. These smaller rocks then break down into pebbles, and finally into very small grains that we call *sand*.

1. Where can you find sand?
2. How does sand feel when it is dry and when it is wet?
3. Why does sand need to be wet when you build with it?
4. What is a sand dollar? Can you buy things with it?
5. What words can you think of that rhyme with **sand?**
6. Sand made from the mineral quartz is a yellow-brown color. What other colors do you think sand can be?

What can people find at a library?

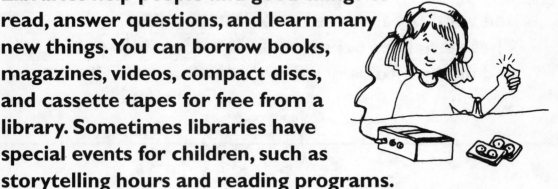

Libraries help people find good things to read, answer questions, and learn many new things. You can borrow books, magazines, videos, compact discs, and cassette tapes for free from a library. Sometimes libraries have special events for children, such as storytelling hours and reading programs.

1. Do you have your own library card? What is the name of your library?
2. What is your favorite section of your library? Why do you like it so much?
3. Why do you need to be quiet in a library?
4. How can you use a library to find out about things?
5. What is a library fine?
6. What does a librarian do?

Are all cats alike?

All cats have some things in common, but they are not all the same. Big wildcats like tigers, lions, and cheetahs hunt for food. House cats don't have to catch their food, but they do like to sneak up on moving objects. All cats have claws. They have special eyes that help them see clearly at night. All cats use their paws, teeth, and tongues to clean their fur.

1. Which wildcats have you seen? Where did you see them?
2. Why do you think house cats like to chase moving things?
3. Have you ever seen a stalking or prowling pet cat? What did it look like and how did it move?
4. How would you move if you were a stalking cat?
5. Name as many words as you can that rhyme with **cat.** How many did you name?
6. Are catfish and catbirds cats that swim and fly?

How do you ride a trike or a bike?

Both tricycles and bicycles have handlebars so you can hold on to them and steer. They also have pedals so you can use your feet to push and make them move. Trikes and bikes are slightly different, though. *Tri* means "three." So a trike has three wheels, a large wheel in the front and two smaller wheels in the back. *Bi* means "two." A bike has two identical wheels, one behind the other.

1. Have you ever ridden a trike or a bike? Was it hard to do?
2. Why is it easier to ride a tricycle than a bicycle?
3. What are training wheels? How are they used?
4. A bicycle that two people can pedal at the same time is called a *tandem bike*. What do you think it looks like?
5. What is a unicycle?
6. On another piece of paper, draw a picture of you and your friends riding trikes and bikes.

Why is the lion called the king of beasts?

In old fables, the adult male lion is often called the king of the beasts because he is very courageous and strong. His loud, deep roar scares other animals. The shaggy mane around his head, neck, and chest makes him look even more frightening. At mealtime, the male lion eats first and gets the biggest portion of food.

1. What does the mane of an adult male lion look like? What do you think it feels like?
2. What does it mean if we say a person is "lionhearted"?
3. What does a lion tamer at the circus do?
4. When someone is given the "lion's share" of something, what do you think that means?
5. What small pet is related to the lion?
6. Make up a story about a family of lions, called a *pride*, that dress and act like humans.

Who are the Eskimos?

Eskimos are people who live in the very cold, icy regions of Alaska, northern Canada, and the island of Greenland. Eskimos wear very warm clothes usually made from fur. Years ago, Eskimos built houses, called *igloos*, made out of blocks of packed snow. Today, some Eskimos still live in igloos, but most live in stone or wood houses that are much warmer. Some Eskimos still hunt for fish and meat to eat, but most Eskimos buy their food in stores.

1. How did Eskimos get their food many years ago?
2. How do *you* keep warm when it is cold outside?
3. Does an igloo melt when an Eskimo family cooks their food? Why or why not?
4. How do Eskimos move around on all that ice and snow?
5. Draw a picture of an igloo on a separate piece of paper.
6. Pretend you and your family live in an igloo. Make up a story about your life.

Why do dogs, cats, and other animals have fur?

Fur is the soft hair that covers and protects the bodies of many *mammals*, or warm-blooded animals. Many furry animals, including some cats and dogs, live outdoors. Their fur helps keep them warm and protects them from rain and cold wind.

1. Point to the animals in the picture that have thick fur. Which animal doesn't have fur? Why?
2. Why do some furry animals grow more hair in winter?
3. Have you ever seen a cat with fur that is all fluffed up on its body? Why does it do this?
4. Besides cats and dogs, what other pets have fur?
5. Why don't we have thick fur all over our bodies like dogs and cats?
6. Make up a story about some cats and dogs that act like people as they wash, comb, brush, and curl their fur!

Why does a bruise look black and blue?

A bruise is like a cut that bleeds underneath your skin. A bruise looks black and blue because you see the blood through a layer of your skin. When you bruise yourself, your skin doesn't break, even though blood vessels under your skin have been broken and some of the blood has seeped out. This part of your body is hurt on the inside. Your dark-colored bruise will only stay this way for a few days. As your blood moves back into the blood vessels, your bruise lightens until it fades away.

1. When you fall and bruise your skin, how does your skin look and feel?
2. What other things in the picture begin with the letter **b?**
3. What do you think you would see if you looked at a bruise with a magnifying glass?
4. What do you think it means if someone's feelings have been bruised?
5. Why might a supermarket not sell bruised fruit?
6. On a separate piece of paper, draw a child with a bruise on his or her arm or leg. What colors will you make the bruise?

One Step Further

At home, ask an adult to give you an apple. Drop the apple on the floor. Do you see a bruise on the apple's skin? Leave the apple for several hours. Then have an adult help you cut the apple open. What happened under the apple's bruised skin? Will this bruise get better and fade away like a bruise on your skin does? Wait a few days and check the apple's bruised skin. What did you find out?

Why do some animals shed their skins?

When snakes and lizards grow, their skin does not grow with them. Unlike our skin, their skin begins to feel small and tight, just as your shoes feel too tight when your feet grow bigger. So snakes and lizards *shed*, or get rid of, their skin. The skin of a snake comes off in one large piece as the snake slithers out of it. The lizard's skin comes off in pieces as its body grows larger.

ZZiP!

1. Why do young snakes and lizards shed their skins more often than older ones?
2. What animals that live underwater shed their hard shells as they grow larger?
3. What do some trees shed or drop off during autumn?
4. When you shed tears, what are you doing?
5. What do dogs and cats shed? How is their shedding different from that of snakes?
6. What does it mean when an adult says, "I need to shed a few pounds"?

How do snakes help us?

Snakes can be helpful to people because they eat mice, rats, and insects that often damage farm crops. Most snakes use their tongues to search for food. They can smell and feel things with their tongues. When it finds food, a snake swallows its food whole, without chewing it first. Its skin stretches as it pulls its prey into its mouth and pushes it down into its body.

1. Why do snakes have teeth? Do they use them to chew their food?
2. How do you think a long, thin snake can swallow a fat rat?
3. Why do some people think snakes feel slimy? Do they? Have you ever felt a snake? How did it feel?
4. Snakes are reptiles. What other reptiles can you name?
5. What do you think a snake dance is?
6. There is a river in the United States called the Snake River. How do you think it got its name?

Where does water in our homes come from?

Some children think water comes directly from the faucets in their homes. But, water is actually sent to your home through long underground pipes, sometimes from a *reservoir*. A reservoir is a special collecting place for water. How does water get to a reservoir? The sun's heat causes water in oceans, lakes, rivers, and streams to rise up as vapor, or steam, into the air where it forms into clouds. When the clouds become filled with water droplets, the water falls to the earth as rain or snow. Some of this water lands in reservoirs where it can be transferred to homes, buildings, and other places for you to use.

1. How are the children in the pictures saving, or conserving, water? How can you save water in your own home?
2. What is frozen water called? What does it feel like?

3. A faucet is a valve you turn to control the flow of water. How many faucets can you find in your home? How many can you find around the outside of your home or apartment building?

4. What does it mean to tread water? Have you ever done this? Is it easy to do?

5. What does it mean when someone says, "My mouth is watering"?

6. Do you think the surface of the earth is covered with more water or more land? How could you find out?

One Step Further

Ask an adult to help you count all the ways you and your family use water during one day. Count everything your family does with water, such as taking a bath or shower, drinking water, and flushing the toilet. Draw a picture for each way your family uses water. How many different pictures will you draw?

How do firefighters save people?

Firefighters are important people who are trained to fight fires, as well as protect and save people and buildings. When they fight fires, they wear special fireproof hats, coats, and boots that keep them from being burned.

1. Why do fire trucks face the street when parked inside the firehouse?
2. Have you ever visited a firehouse? What did you see and who did you meet?
3. Do you have a fire department near where you live? How would you call it in an emergency?
4. What kinds of fire engines are pumper trucks and ladder trucks? How do firefighters use them?
5. Why do fire trucks have sirens? What other types of vehicles have sirens?
6. If fire can be helpful to keep us warm and for cooking our food when we are camping, why is it so dangerous?

Is an electric eel really electric?

Yes! Electric eels are fish that make electricity inside their bodies. This electricity helps them catch food and scare away enemies. An eel's electric shock stuns small sea creatures so they can't move and the eel can eat them. The eel has special organs that allow it to make and store electricity that it can turn on or off, just like a car battery.

1. What is an electric shock? Is it dangerous?
2. Name some other ways you can get an electric shock.
3. What does the color electric blue look like? Why do you think it is called electric?
4. If you are told you have an electric personality, does that mean you shock people just like an electric eel?
5. Name some other sea creatures that eat small fish. How many can you name?
6. How would you draw electricity? Try it on a separate piece of paper.

Do worms have bones?

No. Worms have no bones in their thin, soft bodies. They do not have legs either. They travel by slithering over the ground using tiny hairs to move themselves. Earthworms live just under the ground in damp soil. They move by burrowing tunnels in the ground.

1. Have you ever seen an earthworm? What did it look like?
2. What animals eat worms? Are worms crunchy?
3. Why do you think some people use worms as bait when they go fishing?
4. Why do earthworms come to the top, or surface, of the earth after it rains?
5. What do you think it means if someone worms his or her way into a line of people?
6. How could you slither along the ground like an earthworm? How would you move your body? What would you do with your legs, feet, arms, and hands?

What is an earthquake?

Moving layers of rock under the ground sometimes cause the earth to shake and the ground to crack. Rocks underground are constantly moving. With each tiny movement, pressure builds up as rocks push against each other. After awhile the pressure makes the rocks snap with a big jolt, called an *earthquake*. Many years ago, people in Asia believed that the shaking was caused by a giant tortoise moving under the ground.

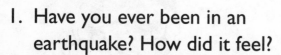

1. Have you ever been in an earthquake? How did it feel?
2. What do you think happens when an earthquake occurs at the bottom of the ocean?
3. What do you think an earthquake sounds like?
4. Why are earthquakes more dangerous in large cities?
5. If you were packing an earthquake survival kit to use after a big quake, what items would you include?
6. On a separate piece of paper, draw a scene showing an earthquake.

Why do people shiver when they get cold?

When our bodies get very cold, our brains tell our muscles to shiver, or shake. This helps warm our bodies as our muscles tighten and relax very quickly over and over again. Each time a muscle moves, it gives off some heat. So as we shiver, we slowly feel warmer.

1. If you were cold and shivering, how could you warm yourself up quickly?
2. Why might your teeth chatter when you are cold?
3. Why do you feel warmer when you ride a bicycle or run?
4. Why might you shiver if you hear a scary story or see a scary movie?
5. How many words can you name that begin with the same **sh** sound as **shiver?**
6. Make up a dance called "The Shiver." Would it be a fast dance or a slow dance?

Is Greenland really green?

No, this big island is almost completely covered with ice. Along some of Greenland's coasts, the ice melts during the warmer parts of the year. Then you can see some green grass, trees, and plants. Over a thousand years ago a Viking explorer named Erik the Red called the frozen island Greenland because he wanted people to think it was good farming land.

1. What do you think might be a better name for Greenland?
2. During what time of the year do you think the coast of Greenland might have green grass and trees?
3. If you were going on a trip to Greenland, what kind of clothing would you bring?
4. Where did the Vikings come from?
5. How could you find out where Greenland is located?
6. What is an island? What other islands are large like Greenland?

Why do some trees lose their leaves in autumn?

In the autumn some trees lose their leaves. Leaves look green in the spring because of a chemical called *chlorophyll*, which plants use to make food. In the fall the chlorophyll starts to disappear. So leaves dry up and their colors turn from green to gold, red, or brown. Finally the dry leaves fall from the trees. This is why autumn is called "fall."

1. What kinds of clothes do people wear in autumn?
2. What are the four seasons?
3. What season is it right now?
4. Fall is pumpkin time. On what two autumn holidays do people use pumpkins?
5. What happens to trees in the spring?
6. How many words can you name that rhyme with **fall**?

What makes the wind blow?

Air temperatures are always changing. This constant change causes the air to move, which makes wind. Air above the hot areas of the earth rises up, and air from cooler areas rushes in to replace it. The more this exchange of hot and cold air takes place, the stronger the wind blows.

1. What happens to tree branches in strong wind?
2. How can you find out if tomorrow will be calm or windy?
3. What does wind sound like?
4. What would happen if you threw a balloon up in the air when there was a light breeze? Would the same thing happen on a windy day? Why or why not?
5. How can you find out if the wind is blowing from the east, west, north, or south?
6. What does it mean if someone says, "It's a very gusty day"?

What is a cavity?

A cavity is a hollow place in a tooth. When you eat, some tiny pieces of food do not go to your stomach. They stay on your teeth. If you don't clean away all the tiny bits of food, a thin, sticky covering called *plaque* forms on your teeth. Plaque has lots of germs in it that slowly eat away at your teeth, which causes cavities.

1. Have you ever had a toothache? What did it feel like?
2. How can you keep plaque from forming on your teeth?
3. What can a dentist do when you have a cavity?
4. What kinds of foods are more likely to cause cavities?
5. On a separate piece of paper, draw what you think a cavity might look like. What color do you think a cavity is?
6. If people are supposed to brush their teeth for three minutes at a time, what can you do to make sure you brush your teeth for the correct amount of time?

What is a shooting star?

A shooting star is really a *meteor*, not a star. Meteors are bits of rock or stardust that fall through space very fast. As they fall, they flash a bright light across the sky that can be seen from great distances. Most shooting stars, or meteors, burn up before they hit the earth. Some land on the ground as chunks of stone or iron.

1. There is a flowering plant called a shooting star. What do you think it looks like?
2. What is a meteor shower? Is it like a shower that you take?
3. When a large meteor lands on earth, it often forms a crater. What do you think a crater is?
4. What might you see when you look up in the sky?
5. Why is it dangerous for a spaceship to fly near a meteor?
6. On a separate piece of paper, draw a shooting star racing through space.

How did the sandwich get its name?

The sandwich was named after the eighteenth-century English nobleman John Montagu, the fourth Earl of Sandwich. The earl loved to play cards, but he didn't always want to leave the game to eat dinner. Eating from a plate of food with a knife and fork at the card table seemed too messy and crowded. So the Earl of Sandwich ordered his servant to bring him two slices of bread with a piece of roast meat between them.

1. When do people usually eat sandwiches?
2. What kind of sandwich do you think was made for the first time in the city of Hamburg, Germany?
3. If you were entering a contest to make the world's best sandwich, what would you put between the two slices of bread?
4. What is a club sandwich? Do you have to belong to a club to eat it?
5. What is your favorite kind of sandwich?
6. If you had a special food named after you, what kind of food would it be? What would it be called?

Why do people get thirsty?

We get thirsty when our bodies do not have enough water to work properly. This happens when we eat salty foods like potato chips or dry foods like crackers. Our mouths feel dry and we get thirsty. We also feel thirsty when we sweat, because we lose a lot of water through our skin. Children should drink at least four glasses of water every day.

1. Why do you need more water on a hot summer day?
2. What kinds of foods make you thirsty?
3. What are your favorite drinks when you get thirsty?
4. Why would you need to drink more water if you were traveling through the desert?
5. If adults should drink two times as much water as children, how many glasses do they need to drink each day?
6. What does it mean when people say someone has a "thirst for knowledge"?

Answers

PAGE 5
1. Answers will vary.
2. Stay inside your house, a building, or a car. Remember thunder cannot hurt us.
3. Child might see lightning, rain, dark clouds, and wind blowing the trees.
4. Sample answers: Writing BOOM! by a lightning flash or drawing a dark cloud.
5. A herd of running elephants sounds very loud, just like thunder.
6. Answers will vary.

PAGE 6
1. Goose bumps don't hurt.
2. Your body may shiver and your teeth may chatter.
3. A large lump is often called a goose egg when it is about the size and shape of a goose's egg.
4. Answers will vary.
5. A gooseneck lamp has a long rod that holds up the lamp. It is flexible like a goose's neck.
6. Answers will vary.

PAGE 7
1. They are both made of iron so they are attracted to each other.
2. A magnet will stick to the refrigerator and other magnets in the picture.
3. A magnet will repel items that do not contain steel or iron.
4. Yes, if it has iron or steel in it.
5. It means the person is fun and people are drawn to him or her.
6. Answers will vary.

PAGE 8
1. Bears like to eat honey.
2. No. A honeycomb is where bees store their honey.
3. Some people call others "honey" because they think the person is sweet like honey.
4. A beekeeper is a person who keeps bees for making honey.
5. A beeline is a straight line or direct route to someplace.
6. Honey tastes sweet. It feels thick and sticky.

PAGE 9
1. The candles, ice cream, and ice will melt.
2. A candle gets smaller as it melts.
3. The butter melts from the heat of the food.
4. Sample answer: Ice cream turns to a liquid when it melts.

5. The opposite of melting is freezing—when a liquid turns into a solid.
6. The sun heats the air, which causes the snow to melt.

PAGES 10–11
1. Child may have seen an opossum in a tree or kangaroos in a zoo.
2. Kangaroos eat grass. They move by hopping on their long back legs.
3. Koalas look like teddy bears. They eat the leaves of eucalyptus trees.
4. Kangaroos and koalas live in Australia.
5. There are five marsupials: two koalas and three kangaroos. There are a total of 14 legs.
6. Answers will vary. *Parent:* Child's drawing should reflect his or her understanding of the text.

PAGE 12
1. Answers will vary.
2. Fog looks like a low cloud that is grayish-white in color. It feels damp on your skin.
3. Because it is hard to see other traffic, the road or sidewalk, people walking, and even traffic lights.
4. The fog surrounding the airport is so thick that airplanes can't safely take off or land.
5. The person means he or she can't think clearly.
6. Answers will vary.

PAGE 13
1. Child should point to chips, soda, cookies, ice cream, and pizza.
2. Healthy foods are apples, grapes, juice, and watermelon.
3–6. Answers will vary.

PAGE 14
1. Answers will vary. *Parent:* Make sure answer reflects child's understanding of text.
2. Answers will vary.
3. Houseflies are insects that are found in and around houses.
4. The fly's legs, feet, body, head, and two see-through wings.
5. Frogs and spiders eat flies.
6. Answers will vary.

PAGE 15
1. Sample answers: Snuggling with an adult while reading a bedtime story and changing into pajamas.
2. Your eyes are shut when you sleep. You move so you won't get sore.

3. Answers will vary. Most young children sleep 10 to 12 hours a night.
4. You are beginning to feel very tired and sleepy.
5. You have trouble falling asleep when your brain is too excited and can't slow down and rest.
6. You may feel tired, grouchy, or even irritable.

PAGES 16–17
1. The tennis ball, life vests, boat and a duck will float.
2. The rock and sponge will sink.
3. People can float by lying very still and straight on their backs, or by sitting or lying on an inner tube or raft.
4. Sample answers: boat, coat, goat, moat. The boat and the goat can float.
5. Sample answers: Blink, ink, link, stink, and wink rhyme with **sink.**
6. A floating island is made of a large mass of earth that is floating on top of the water.

PAGE 18
1. Answers will vary.
2. Hiccups make a loud, funny sound.
3. Sample answer: You can quickly drink a tall glass of water. Usually they will stop on their own after a few minutes.
4. Answers will vary.
5. A hiccup happens when you breathe in a lot of air. A cough clears the windpipe by pushing out air from the lungs.
6. Answers will vary.

PAGE 19
1. Answers will vary.
2. Sample answers: The magical parts, such as when animals talk, show that fairy tales are make-believe.
3–6. Answers will vary.

PAGE 20
1–2. Answers will vary.
3. To daydream means to think about pleasant things while you are still awake. You can daydream at night or during the day.
4. The child in the picture is daydreaming about going to an amusement park and riding on a roller coaster.
5. Nightmares are scary dreams. Rest of answer will vary.
6. Answers will vary.

PAGE 21

1. The children are climbing the tree, swinging from a swing, and reading in the shade.
2. Sample answers: Trees give people oxygen to breathe, fruit to eat, and shade.
3. Sample answers: apples, bananas, oranges, cherries, pears, walnuts, almonds, and pecans.
4. Sample answers: Caterpillars, koalas, deer, elephants, giraffes, and porcupines eat the leaves of trees. Elephants, squirrels, beavers, and orangutans eat the bark of trees.
5. Sample answers: monkeys, birds, squirrels, tree frogs, and honeybees.
6. Answers will vary.

PAGE 22

1. The stripes on its fur help it blend into its surroundings.
2. The cheetah and leopard.
3. Female birds' feathers are usually the same colors as their surroundings so they can hide when caring for their babies.
4. Sample answers: bears, lions, tigers, chameleons, ants, worms, rabbits, and mice.
5–6. Answers will vary.

PAGE 23

1. Answers will vary.
2. Sour lemon juice is tasted on the middle sides of the tongue. Salty potato chips are tasted on the front tip of the tongue.
3. It means the food has lots of flavor and tastes good.
4. Salt, pepper, and sugar make foods taste stronger. The front sides of your tongue taste sugar.
5. It means you can pick out clothes that look nice together.
6. Answers will vary.

PAGE 24

1. They are making shadow pictures of a monster by moving their hands between the light and the wall.
2. You can make a shadow of yourself by standing with the sun or a light shining on your back.
3. No. Because there is no sun to create a shadow.
4. Answers will vary.
5. It means someone is following behind a person very closely.
6. Answers will vary.

PAGE 25

1. A cow can be seen on a farm, in a pasture, or at a county or state fair.
2. Cows are taller than young children. They have white, brown, or black hair. Sometimes they have two colors or large spots.
3. A herd.
4. Cows produce milk and meat.
5. Cows swish their tails back and forth very quickly like a flyswatter to keep insects away.
6. You have two calves on your body. They are the lower back parts of your leg.

PAGE 26

1. It would fall down.
2.

jawbone
collarbone
backbone
thighbone
shinbone
anklebone

3. The skull.
4. The X ray takes pictures of your bones.
5. Answers will vary.
6. This means a person is very thin and it is easy to see and feel the person's bones through his or her skin.

PAGE 27

1. The child cut himself. The adult is cleaning the cuts.
2. Answers will vary.
3. The scab may be knocked off too early and the cut may not heal properly.
4. Pus is made by the antibodies that fight infection inside the body.
5. Cats and dogs also bleed when they cut themselves.
6. Bandages help stop bleeding and protect cuts from dirt and infection.

PAGES 28–29

1. They are putting plastic, glass, newspapers, and aluminum into recycling bins.
2. Sample answer: You can scatter small pieces on the ground for birds to eat.
3. Answers will vary.
4. Old tires can be used for swings or to climb on.
5. Sample answers: Some newspapers, greeting cards, grocery bags, writing paper, and books are made from recycled materials.
6. Answers will vary.

PAGE 30

1. Nerve endings in the skin help you touch. You hear with your ears.
2. You are using your sense of sight, hearing, and touch.
3. All five senses are working when eating a crunchy apple. You see the apple with your eyes, feel it with your hands, taste it with your taste buds, hear its crunch with your ears, and smell it with your nose.
4. A cold often makes it hard to smell things, because your nose gets stuffed up.
5. You use all of your senses to learn.
6. Answers will vary.

PAGE 31

1. Sample answers: Museums often have dinosaur skeletons. Rest of answer will vary.
2. Sample answers: stegosaurus, velocorapter, and triceratops.
3. No. Dinosaurs died out millions of years before human beings appeared on earth.
4. Lizards, snakes, turtles, alligators, and snakes are reptiles living today.
5. Many zoos have a reptile house. You can also find reptiles living in many parts of the world.
6. Extinct means that the dinosaurs died out and they are gone from the earth forever.

PAGE 32

1. Answers will vary.
2. Your nose can't run like you because it doesn't have legs or feet!
3. You can give a friend a tissue or a handkerchief.
4. A runny nose drips mucus just like a dripping faucet drips water.
5. Yes. Dogs, cats, and horses get runny noses when they get colds.
6. Answers will vary.

PAGE 33

1. People get milk from a cow by milking it by hand or attaching a milking machine to the cow's udder.
2. Sample answers: cheese, butter, yogurt, and ice cream.
3. Answers will vary.
4. Sample answers: how, now, pow, vow, and bowwow.
5. Once the cow is milked, the milk is taken to a large building where it is processed and put into milk containers. It is then shipped to stores where people buy it.
6. Sample answers: People also drink

milk from goats, camels, llamas, sheep, and buffalos. Rest of answer will vary.

PAGE 34

1. Sample answer: The skin probably looked and felt bumpy.
2. They have been swimming. They are laughing at their funny-looking wrinkled toes and fingers.
3. Dried fruits like prunes, raisins, and apricots all have wrinkled skins.
4. As people get older, their skin loses some of its fullness, and wrinkles.
5. Sample answers: People can try to shake or iron out the wrinkles.
6. Answers will vary.

PAGE 35

1. You can find sand at the beach, in a sandbox, and in the desert.
2. Sand feels grainy when dry. It feels gritty and mushy when wet.
3. It needs to be wet so the grains will hold together in a shape.
4. A sand dollar is a small flat sea urchin. You can't buy anything with a sand dollar!
5. Sample answers: and, hand, band, and land.
6. Sand can be white, black, gold, or gray.

PAGE 36

1–2. Answers will vary.
3. It is hard to concentrate or read if it is noisy.
4. You can learn about things from books, magazines, videos, the computer, and reference books.
5. A library fine is the money you pay for overdue library books and other borrowed library materials.
6. A librarian helps people find information.

PAGE 37

1. Sample answers: Wild cats such as lions, tigers, leopards, and panthers can be seen at a zoo or wild animal park.
2. They like to chase moving objects for fun.
3–4. Answers will vary.
5. Sample answers: at, bat, brat, fat, flat, gnat, hat, mat, pat, rat, sat, spat, and that.
6. No. A catfish is a fish that has long feelers by its mouth that look like a cat's whiskers. A catbird is a bird that makes a crying sound very much like a cat's meow.

PAGE 38

1. Answers will vary.
2. Tricycles are easier to ride because they have three wheels, which make them balanced.
3. Two training wheels placed on either side of the rear wheel of a bicycle help keep the bike upright.
4. A tandem bike has two wheels, two seats, and two sets of handle-bars and pedals, placed one in back of the other.
5. A unicycle has only one wheel with two pedals, a seat, and no handlebars.
6. Answers will vary.

PAGE 39

1. The mane is the long, shaggy, and thick hair around the head, neck, and chest of the adult male lion. Rest of answer will vary.
2. To be "lionhearted" means the person is very courageous.
3. A lion tamer trains lions to do special tricks.
4. When someone gets the lion's share of something he or she has the biggest and best piece.
5. A cat.
6. Answers will vary.

PAGE 40

1. Eskimos had to hunt and fish for food to eat.
2. Answers will vary.
3. No. The snow blocks of the igloo are very thick and the temperature is so cold that the igloo doesn't melt from cooking.
4. Eskimos use snowmobiles, sleds pulled by dogs, and snowshoes to move on the snow and ice. They use kayaks and motor boats to travel on water.
5. Answers will vary. An igloo is a dome-shaped hut made from blocks of hard, packed snow.
6. Answers will vary.

PAGE 41

1. The monkey and tiger have fur. The pig is covered with coarse bristles.
2. To keep them warm during the cold winter.
3. When a cat is scared, it will lower its tail, arch its back, and fluff out its hair.
4. Sample answers: rabbits, hamsters, mice, guinea pigs, and horses.
5. We don't need fur to protect us. We use clothes to keep us warm and dry.
6. Answers will vary.

PAGES 42–43

1. Answers will vary.
2. Sample answers: bike, ball, bat, belt, basket, bunny, book, boy, bow, banana, and buttons.
3. Sample answers: A bruise would look bluish-purple. You may see some veins in the bruise.
4. It means that their feelings have been hurt.
5. Bruised fruit is damaged and will not taste good.
6. Answers will vary.

PAGE 44

1. Because they are growing.
2. Crabs and lobsters shed their shells as they grow.
3. Some trees shed their leaves.
4. You are crying.
5. Dogs and cats shed their old hair a little bit at a time, not all at once, like a snake.
6. This means the person wants to lose some weight.

PAGE 45

1. Snakes use their teeth to grab and hold their food, not to chew it.
2. The snake's loosely attached jawbones allow its mouth to open very wide to swallow something big for dinner.
3. When a snake is in the sun, its skin shines so much it almost looks wet. A snake's skin isn't slimy. It is dry and feels a little like leather. Rest of answer will vary.
4. Sample answers: lizards, crocodiles, and turtles.
5. A snake dance is performed by a long line of people who twist their way around a room. It is also a ceremonial Native American dance using snakes.
6. From above, the Snake River looks like a snake.

PAGES 46–47

1. By putting drinking water in the refrigerator to keep it cold instead of letting the water run from the faucet; sweeping the patio instead of hosing it with water; turning off a dripping faucet.
2. Frozen water is called ice. It feels hard and cold.
3. Answers will vary.
4. To tread water means you are swimming in an upright position without moving forward. Rest of answer will vary.
5. This means a person's mouth is drooling saliva.

6. The earth's surface is covered with more than 70% water. You can find this information in an encyclopedia, in books about the earth, or on a map of the world.

PAGE 48
1. So they can be driven out of the firehouse very quickly.
2–3. Answers will vary.
4. A pumper truck carries a pump and hoses used to spray water. The ladder truck carries long ladders to help firefighters reach tall buildings and rescue people.
5. So people will get out of their way and they can get to the fires faster. Police cars and ambulances also have sirens.
6. Fire is dangerous because it can spread fast, get out of control, and possibly hurt you.

PAGE 49
1. An electric shock is electricity passing through your body. It is very dangerous and can burn you.
2. You can get an electric shock if you touch the inside of a toaster with a metal fork or if you use an appliance like a hair dryer with wet hands. **Never do this!**
3. Electric blue is a very bright, shiny, or metallic blue color. It looks like the blue flash of electricity.
4. No. It means you are a fun and exciting person.
5. Sample answers: shark, octopuses, and stingrays. Rest of answer will vary.
6. Answers will vary.

PAGE 50
1. Answers will vary.
2. Some birds, frogs, and fish eat worms. Worms aren't crunchy because they have no bones.
3. Fish will eat worms. Some people think the wiggling worms attract fish in search of food.
4. So they will not be flooded out by all the water entering their homes.
5. It means the person is creeping into the line in front of someone else.
6. Answers will vary.

PAGE 51
1. Answers will vary.
2. It causes large, dangerous waves.
3. An earthquake makes a loud rumbling sound like a rushing train.

4. Large cities have many tall buildings, highways, and bridges that may collapse.
5. Sample answers: bottled water, canned and dried foods, a first aid kit, a flashlight, extra clothing and shoes, blankets, toilet paper, a portable radio, and batteries.
6. Answers will vary.

PAGE 52
1. Sample answers: By putting on warm clothing, covering yourself with a blanket, or by jumping up and down.
2. Because your jaw muscles are moving quickly as your body is trying to warm itself.
3. You feel warmer when you exercise because your muscles are working harder and moving faster.
4. Because your body is chilled by the scary things you hear or see.
5. There are many, many words that begin with the **sh** sound.
6. Answers will vary.

PAGE 53
1. Answers will vary.
2. During the summer.
3. You should pack warm clothes for a trip to Greenland.
4. They came from the Scandinavian countries in Northern Europe.
5. Look at a map or a globe of the world.
6. A mass of land surrounded by water. Other very large islands include: New Guinea, Borneo, Madagascar, Australia, and Iceland.

PAGE 54
1. People usually wear warmer clothes, including sweaters and jackets.
2. Winter, spring, summer, and autumn (fall).
3. Answers will vary.
4. People use pumpkins on Halloween and at Thanksgiving.
5. They grow new leaves.
6. Sample answers: all, ball, call, hall, mall, small, stall, tall, and wall.

PAGE 55
1. They will move or sway.
2. Listening to the radio, watching the news, or reading a newspaper.
3. Wind can howl or make leaves rustle together.

4. In a light wind, the balloon would float gently on the air currents. On a windy day, the balloon would fly around very fast.
5. You can use a compass or a weather vane.
6. On a gusty day, the wind is blowing with sudden bursts or gusts of air, not in a steady stream.

PAGE 56
1. Answers will vary.
2. By brushing and flossing your teeth.
3. A dentist can fill the cavity so the soft center is protected.
4. Sweet, sugary foods.
5. Answers will vary.
6. You can use an hourglass, a timer, a stopwatch, or a clock.

PAGE 57
1. It is a plant that has clusters of star-shaped blossoms.
2. It is a flash of light made by falling meteors.
3. A crater is a large hole formed in the earth.
4. The sun, moon, and stars.
5. It may be hit and damaged by the meteor rock.
6. Answers will vary.

PAGE 58
1. Many people eat sandwiches for lunch.
2. A hamburger.
3. Answers will vary.
4. A traditional club sandwich is made with three or more slices of toast filled with lettuce, bacon, tomatoes, turkey, and mayonnaise. No, you don't have to belong to a club to eat it!
5–6. Answers will vary.

PAGE 59
1. Your body needs to replace the water it loses when you sweat on a hot day.
2. Salty and dry foods will make you thirsty.
3. Answers will vary.
4. The hot, dry desert air makes you sweat and lose water.
5. Adults need eight glasses of water each day.
6. It means a person is eager to learn new things.

Other **GIFTED & TALENTED®**

books that will help develop your child's gifts and talents

Workbooks:
- Reading (4–6) $3.95
- Math (4–6) $3.95
- Language Arts (4–6) $3.95
- Puzzles & Games for
  Reading and Math (4–6) $3.95
- Puzzles & Games for
  Critical and Creative Thinking (4–6) $3.95
- Reading Book Two (4–6) $3.95
- Math Book Two (4–6) $3.95
- Phonics (4–6) $4.95
- Math Puzzles & Games (4–6) $4.95
- Reading Puzzles & Games (4–6) $4.95
- Math (6–8) $3.95
- Language Arts (6–8) $3.95
- Puzzles & Games for
  Reading and Math (6–8) $3.95
- Puzzles & Games for
  Critical and Creative Thinking (6–8) $3.95
- Puzzles & Games for
  Reading and Math, Book Two (6–8) $3.95
- Phonics (6–8) $4.95
- Reading Comprehension (6–8) $4.95

Reference Workbooks:
- Word Book (4–6) $3.95
- Almanac (6–8) $3.95

- Atlas (6–8) $3.95
- Dictionary (6–8) $3.95

Story Starters:
- My First Stories (6–8) $3.95
- Stories About Me (6–8) $3.95

Question & Answer Books:
- The Gifted & Talented® Question & Answer
  Book for Ages 4–6 $5.95
- The Gifted & Talented® Question & Answer
  Book for Ages 6–8 $5.95
- Gifted & Talented® More Questions &
  Answers for Ages 4–6 $5.95

Drawing Books:
- Learn to Draw (6 and up) $5.95

Readers:
- Double the Trouble (6–8) $7.95
- Time for Bed (6–8) $7.95

For Parents:
- How to Develop Your Child's Gifts and
  Talents During the Elementary Years $11.95
- How to Develop Your Child's Gifts and
  Talents in Math $12.95
- How to Develop Your Child's Gifts and
  Talents in Reading $12.95

Available where good books are sold! **or** *Send a check or money order, plus shipping charges, to:*

Handy Worksheet

Department JH
Lowell House
2029 Century Park East, Suite 3290
Los Angeles, CA 90067

For special or bulk sales, call (800) 552-7551, EXT 112

Note: Minimum order of three titles. **On a separate piece of paper,**
please specify exact titles and ages and include a breakdown of costs, as follows:

(# of books) ____	x $3.95	= ____	(Subtotal) = ____
(# of books) ____	x $4.95	= ____	*California residents*
(# of books) ____	x $5.95	= ____	*add 8.25% sales tax* = ____
(# of books) ____	x $7.95	= ____	Shipping charges
(# of books) ____	x $11.95	= ____	(# of books) ____ x $1.00/ book = ____
(# of books) ____	x $12.95	= ____	**Total cost** = ____